THE NIGHT BEFORE
CHRISTMAS
in Paris

BETTY LOU PHILLIPS
AND ROBLYN HERNDON

ILLUSTRATED BY

SHERYL DICKERT

GIBBS SMITH
TO ENRICH AND INSPIRE HUMANKIND

Twas the week before Christmas!
    All over the world
The children were breathless
    as visions unfurled
Of the magical time when their
    dreams would take flight
And the sweet sound of sleigh bells
    would ring in the night.

But Santa was frantic—
    he wasn't elated,
For his dear Mrs. Claus
    could not be located.
The lists were not finished;
    the maps were a mess,
And where to deliver
    was anyone's guess.

Santa's sweet wife
    was indeed indispensable.
To question her value
    was quite reprehensible.
She took care of Santa,
    the man she revered.
She ironed his red outfit and
    trimmed his white beard.

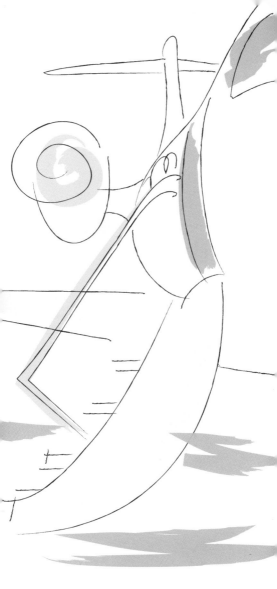

But she'd flown off to Paris
one day in September
For a Fashion Week peek and
she'd vowed to remember
To fly back at once
after sampling the food,
Enhancing her wardrobe,
and lifting her mood.

Three months and counting,
and nothing was heard.
Not a call, not a tweet, not a text—
not a word!
St. Nicholas knew that his
choice was quite clear:
"I have to go find her and
bring her back here."

So late that dark evening
  his reindeer he drew
To the sleigh, and took off
  before anyone knew.
They flew like a flash,
  and the ocean rushed by.
The stars overhead
  lit their path through the sky.

"**D**o you think I could miss it
and end up in Spain?
No, there's no chance of that
if I steer by the Seine.
And Paris stands out,
for it sparkles a lot.
The City of Light will be
easy to spot!"

"I'll look for a landmark,"
    he heard himself say.
"The tall Eiffel Tower
    will show us the way."
He rapidly planned
    his descent in the sleigh
And glided to earth on the
    Champs-Élysées.

The Louvre is the first place that everyone seeks.
Within its wide halls she could wander for weeks!
Mais non, she'd move on once she'd seen Mona Lisa,
With Paris before her, she'd pull out her VISA.

The Tuileries Gardens?
No, not in the dark.
The Bateaux Mouches tours?
It's too cold to embark.
The Musée d'Orsay?
She could never go wrong
In Impressionist heaven!

But not for this long!

The Carnavalet! That has
  well-deserved fame.
The Île de la Cité, where we
  find Notre-Dame.
All Paris I'll check, from
  the hub to the rim.
I have but one goal, and that's
  'Cherchez la femme!'

The Faubourg Saint-Honoré
glitters with fashion
I know she'd be tempted,
    for that is her passion.
Happily sated with
    couture and art
She'd head for the Left Bank,
    or maybe Montmartre.

No wait! I've the answer!
She'd have a brief rest
In her *haute* hotel suite,
  which I'm sure is the best.
She'd circle the fabulous
  Rue de la Paix,
The Place Vendôme windows
  she'd catch on the way.

So it's on to the Ritz,
    where a doorman would loom
To fling wide the door,
    and she'd head to her room.
Mon Dieu! She's not here.
    I am knocking in vain.
Am I doomed to explore
    the whole city again?

I've got it! I'll look for a
palace of sweets
Like Ladurée's macarons—
   those are delightful treats.
I'll check Angelina's—
   oh, isn't this great—
There she is—eating *chocolat!*

She rushes to meet him,
her arms open wide.
"I've missed you, my dearest.
  Come sit down inside!
You never could guess all the
  sights that I've viewed.
Have a sweet, and we'll eat as you
  tell me the news."

"Here it is," said Saint Nick,
  "Right down to the letter,
The North Pole awaits us—
    the sooner the better!
So let's have a night we may
    never repeat,
A Tour d'Argent table for two,
    and *bon nuit!*

"We'll fill our Champagne flutes
and toast to the end
Of a lovely adventure.
    We'll tell every friend
That the magic of Paris is
    just what you need
To discover there's magic in
    Christmas indeed!"

Her Louis Vuittons were
   all ready to go.
The reindeer were waiting,
   impatiently so.
"Mission accomplished!
   No longer we'll roam!
Dasher and Dancer, we're
   on the way home!"

After loading the sleigh to the brim with each treasure,
They flew like the wind
   and the trip was a pleasure.
The landing was gentle,
   the future was bright.
A star-studded end to a
   wonderful night.

The countdown to Christmas
  was now underway.
The elves were all willing;
  they toiled night and day.
When Mrs. Claus chose for
  the girls and the boys,
She donned her Chanel to pick
  just the right toys.

Saint Nicholas smiled at the
thought of each child
At the foot of the Christmas tree,
presents all piled.
His memories were sweet of the
City of Light.

Happy Christmas to All

and to All a Good Night!

First Edition
16 15 14 13   5 4 3

Published by
Gibbs Smith
P.O. Box 667
Layton, Utah 84041

1.800.835.4993 orders
www.gibbs-smith.com

Designed and illustrated by Sheryl Dickert
Printed and bound in China
Gibbs Smith books are printed on either
recycled, 100% post-consumer waste, FSC-
certified papers or on paper produced from
sustainable PEFC-certified forest/controlled
wood source. Learn more at www.pefc.org.

Library of Congress Cataloging-
in-Publication Data

Phillips, Betty Lou.
  The night before Christmas in Paris /
Betty Lou Phillips and Roblyn Herndon ;
illustrated by Sheryl Dickert. — 1st ed.
      p. cm.
  ISBN 978-1-4236-3053-1
1. Christmas—Poetry. 2. Paris
(France)—Poetry. I. Herndon, Roblyn.
II. Dickert, Sheryl. III. Title.
  PS3616.H453N54 2012
  811'.6—dc23
                              2012006757